# Fairy Tale
# Twists

For my own lovely
literary Fairy Godmothers,
Sara, Sara, Catherine and Jenny x
K.D.

For Emily
M.B.

Reading Consultant: Prue Goodwin, Lecturer in literacy and children's books

ORCHARD BOOKS
338 Euston Road, London NW1 3BH
*Orchard Books Australia*
Level 17/207 Kent Street, Sydney, NSW 2000

First published in 2012
First paperback publication in 2013

ISBN 978 1 40831 215 5 (hardback)
ISBN 978 1 40831 223 0 (paperback)

A CIP catalogue record for this book is available
from the British Library.

1 3 5 7 9 10 8 6 4 2 (hardback)
1 3 5 7 9 10 8 6 4 2 (paperback)

Printed in Great Britain

Orchard Books is a division of Hachette Children's Books,
an Hachette UK company.

www.hachette.co.uk

# Fairy Tale Twists

## The Unfair-y Godmother

Written by Katie Dale
Illustrated by Matt Buckingham

ORCHARD

For Emma
& Abby

Happy Reading!
Love,
Katie Dale
xx

What's your favourite fairy story?
Tales of love? Or something gory?
Princesses in caves and towers,
or witches with amazing powers?

Dragons, mermaids, elves or bears?
A slipper left upon the stairs?
Fairies? Giants? Towering beds?
Or big bad wolves and trolls instead?

You've had the books since you were small,
but do you know who *wrote* them all?
Hans Anderson, you say? Not him.
Not Disney, nor the Brothers Grimm.

The *fairy* tales are by no other…
than me, of course – Fairy Godmother!

Fluttering over hills and streams,
I spend my days fulfilling dreams.
Then write the tales behind the wishes
(often while I do the dishes).

I wasn't always a godmother –
just a sprite like any other.
Then one fateful day the king
said: "Bless my daughter's christening!"

I stood before the joyful crowd,
feeling honoured, thrilled and proud –
till I discovered that two others
*also* had been made godmothers!

"My present is the gift of song!"
announced Godmother Number One.
"She'll sing as sweetly as a bird –
the finest voice you've ever heard."

My present of a magic ball
suddenly felt rather small.

I glanced at Godmum Number Two.
"Oh, please," I told her. "After you."

"The gift of beauty is my choice,
to complement her stunning voice.
With big blue eyes and golden hair,
her looks will be beyond compare."

"Your turn, deary," smiled the king.
"Oh cripes!" I muttered, panicking.
"I can't!" I mumbled. "Wait, I mean—"
Just then…

# "Intruder!" screamed the queen.

"The Wicked Witch!" The crowd went wild.
Her Highness grabbed the crying child.
I seized my chance – I had to cheat –
what gift would make her life complete?

I shook the magic ball of gold:
"What does this baby's future hold?"
The girl appeared, sweet-voiced and fair,
I watched the image in despair…

But when the girl began to chatter
all around began to scatter!
She was dull as dirty water!

"Quick!" the king cried. "Help my
  daughter!
The witch sent her to sleep forever!"
"Blimey!" I thought. "That was clever!
If all she does is sleep and snore,
they'll never know she's such a bore!"

"Oh *can* you help?" the queen begged.

"Well…
you know I can't *undo* the spell,
but Majesties, don't be dismayed!
She may sleep more than other maids…
but she'll awake to True Love's Kiss,
and wed a prince, and live in bliss."

I flicked my wand.

"Hip-hip-hooray!"
the king rejoiced. "You've saved the day!"
The news spread quickly through the land
and soon I was in great demand!

The problem is that ever since,
they ALL expect to wed a prince!

It might sound like a cushy job –
I flick my wand and, like a slob,
the spell is done – no work, no stress,
no damage to my sparkly dress.
(The dress *is* fab – the wings are great –
especially if I'm running late!)

But it's not always quite that simple;
*anyone* can fix a pimple…
Looks are easy, brains are not –
I have to work with what I've got.
I can't make maidens sweet or witty,
but, by gosh, I'll make 'em pretty!

All the really stupid girls
I give blue eyes and glossy curls.
Then when I've made them tall and slim
most princes *don't care* that they're dim!

It sometimes works the other way.
For instance, just the other day,
young Cinderella's dad got wed.
She gained two sisters – Belle and Red.

These lovely twins were kind and fair –
poor Cinders just could not compare.
"Oh help me, Godmother!" she cried.
"Make Rose-Red ugly! Make Belle wide!"

I flicked my wand – they both turned ugly.
Spiteful Cinders giggled smugly.
I had no choice but to support her –
after all, she's my goddaughter.

And though I've wings and magic powers,
I can never *choose* my hours.
For instance, on an average day,
I'll grant a dozen wishes, say.
For these, I rush throughout the land,
my trusty wand gripped in my hand.

Then there are weddings, births and balls,
and lightning, hurricanes and squalls!

Till finally it's time for bed –
but no, I write my tales instead,
and drop off at ten-thirty-ish…

Then **BAM**, somebody makes a wish!

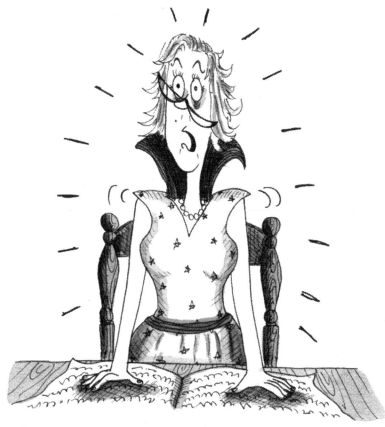

I listen to them sob and weep
(while trying not to fall asleep).
But this can go on *all night long* –
especially if things go wrong!

Just after twelve I got a call
from Cinders, stranded at the ball!

So, tired and grumpy, off I flew.
The rain poured down, the north wind
blew...

I'm sick of this, I'm getting old –
*why can't young girls do as they're told?*
"Remember, don't stay past midnight!"
Did Cinders listen? Or Snow White?

"Just stay inside! Don't talk to strangers!"
*Crumbs!* You'd think they *welcomed*
  dangers!
And so I let them sweat – that way
next time they'll do just as I say.

After all, it serves them right
to walk home in the dead of night…

…or sleep a while and – saints above! –
think that a *dwarf* is Snow's true love!

I always fix it – I'm not *mean* –
young Cinders still became a queen.

Likewise, I'll visit Snow tonight –
I'll wave my wand and put things right.

The "True Love's Kiss" thing works
  quite well –
it's actually my favourite spell.
If girls are *really* dull or dumb,
they sleep until a prince can come.

But sometimes it's just not enough.
Boys like to prove that they are tough.
They jump at any chance to save
a maiden from a tower or cave.

Then add to this a monstrous beast –
a dragon at the very least.
Mix in a swamp, an eerie mist –
they flock for miles! They can't resist!

Of course, to carry out this scheme
these weird creatures need to seem…
scary! Terrifying! Vicious!
*So what* if it's just fictitious…?

For who'd be scared of the Phil the ogre
if they saw him doing yoga?

Likewise, crossword-loving Dylan
hardly makes a creepy villain.

These "monsters" wouldn't scare a fly –
so what's a teensy little lie…?
It all works out – the beasts get fed,
the boys feel brave, my girls get wed…

If princes *don't* co-operate,

I get an *eensy* bit irate...

I start to shake, I cough and choke,

my breath comes out in thick black

smoke...

I find a month spent as a frog
within a slimy, stinky bog
is quite a good way to convince
all but the most *reluctant* prince.

And, in a most delicious twist,
*they're* now begging to be kissed!

Yes, now and then boys need a nudge –
but if they *still* refuse to budge…

Well, look at young Pinocchio –
the brat refused to kiss my Snow…

"Release me! I'm a real boy!"

"Not any more – you're just
a toy!"

Since time began, and ever since,
the heroine *must* wed a prince!
If anyone stands in my way
then golly gosh, I'll make them—

"**HEY!** Stop that frog! He's got
my wand!"

Frog hopped away towards the pond…
He flicked it once and with a *CRACK!*
*all* the princes turned straight back!

But then he turned my wand on me!

"Now, which would you prefer to be –
a frog, a leech, or slimy toad?
Let's see how *you* like it," he crowed.

With that he snapped my wand in half!

"OH *NO*! How *will* I save Snow White?
She's set to wed a *dwarf* tonight!"

"Then let it be!" the prince replied.
"For – look! She'll make a happy bride!"
He shook my ball, I stared in awe
at what Snow's future held in store…

For sure enough, she looked ecstatic.

"Money isn't everything –
nor's marrying a prince or king.
Just look at Bella, look at Red –
they all live happily!" he said.

"But, honey – that's my whole career! Without my spells, I'm just – well – tragic! What's a fairy without magic?"

"Magic's not *all* you do well," he grinned. "And you'll still need to spell…"

"I don't understand," I sniffed.

"Your *stories* are your greatest gift!
For *everybody* reads your books!
Princesses, paupers, kings and crooks…
For *you* tell stories like no other –
you're the great Fairy Godmother!
Write more books – but tell the truth!"

"You mean what *really* happened?
Strewth!"

And so I wrote this very series
telling you the truth, my dearies —
how the witch is really nice…

what happened to those three blind
mice…

The hidden tales of Cinderella,
Goldilocks, the Wolf, and Bella…

Charming, Jack, the old Stepmother,
and even me, Fairy Godmother.

And do they all end happily…?
That *would* be telling – wait and see…

# Fairy Tale Twists

## Written by Katie Dale
## Illustrated by Matt Buckingham

All priced at £4.99

Orchard Books are available from all good bookshops,
or can be ordered from our website, www.orchardbooks.co.uk,
or telephone 01235 827702, or fax 01235 827703.